Our Exciting Earth!

RAINFORESTS

By Jagger Youssef

Gareth Stevens
PUBLISHING

Please visit our website, www.garethstevens.com. For a free color catalog of all our high-quality books, call toll free 1-800-542-2595 or fax 1-877-542-2596.

Cataloging-in-Publication Data

Names: Youssef, Jagger.
Title: Rainforests / Jagger Youssef.
Description: New York : Gareth Stevens Publishing, 2018. | Series: Our exciting Earth! | Includes index.
Identifiers: ISBN 9781538209776 (pbk.) | ISBN 9781538209790 (library bound) | ISBN 9781538209783 (6 pack)
Subjects: LCSH: Rain forest ecology–Juvenile literature. | Rain forests–Juvenile literature.
Classification: LCC QH541.5.R27Y68 2018 | DDC 577.34–dc23

Published in 2018 by
Gareth Stevens Publishing
111 East 14th Street, Suite 349
New York, NY 10003

Editor: Therese Shea
Designer: Bethany Perl

Photo credits: Cover, p. 1 soft_light/Shutterstock.com; p. 5 Sarah Winter/Shutterstock.com; p. 7 4FR/E+/Getty Images; p. 9 Gustavo Frazao/Shutterstock.com; p. 11 Ryan M. Bolton/Shutterstock.com; p. 13 i viewfinder/Shutterstock.com; p. 15 ProDesign studio/Shutterstock.com; p. 17 Iammotos/Shutterstock.com; pp. 19, 24 OlegD/Shutterstock.com; pp. 21, 24 Dirk Ercken/Shutterstock.com; pp. 23, 24 herjua/Shutterstock.com.

Printed in the United States of America

CPSIA compliance information: Batch #CW18GS: For further information contact Gareth Stevens, New York, New York at 1-800-542-2595.

Contents

Let's go to a rainforest!

All rainforests get a lot of rain.

The biggest one is in Brazil.

Half of all kinds of plants and animals live in rainforests.

We go to a rainforest.
It’s rainy!

There are tall trees.
They block the sun.

Some plants grow up trees. They want to reach light!

Foods grow
in rainforests.
I see bananas!

I see lots of animals.
Hello, tree frog!

Let's hike!
Rainforests are fun!

Words to Know

bananas

hike

tree frog

Index